To. Joseph
from. mommy

HECTOR PROTECTOR
AND
AS I WENT OVER THE WATER

HECTOR PROTECTOR
AND
AS I WENT OVER THE WATER

TWO NURSERY RHYMES WITH PICTURES
BY
MAURICE SENDAK

A TRUMPET CLUB SPECIAL EDITION

Published by The Trumpet Club
666 Fifth Avenue, New York, New York 10103

ISBN: 0-440-84342-1

This edition published by arrangement with
HarperCollins Publishers
Printed in the United States of America
September 1991

10 9 8 7 6 5 4 3 2 1
UPC

Hector Protector was dressed all in green.

Hector Protector was sent to the queen.

The queen did not like him

no more did the king

so Hector Protector was sent back again.

As I went over the water

the water went over me.

I saw two little blackbirds sitting on a tree.

One called me a rascal

and one called me a thief.

I took up my little black stick

and knocked out all their teeth !